HOSTAGE RESCUE WITH THE FBI

Rescue and Prevention: Defending Our Nation

- Biological and Germ Warfare Protection
- Border and Immigration Control
- Counterterrorist Forces with the CIA
- The Department of Homeland Security
- The Drug Enforcement Administration
- Firefighters
- Hostage Rescue with the FBI
- The National Guard
- Police Crime Prevention
- Protecting the Nation with the U.S. Air Force
- Protecting the Nation with the U.S. Army
- Protecting the Nation with the U.S. Navy
- Rescue at Sea with the U.S. and Canadian Coast Guards
- The U.S. Transportation Security Administration
- Wilderness Rescue with the U.S. Search and Rescue Task Force

RESCUE AND PREVENTION: Defending Our Nation

HOSTAGE RESCUE WITH THE FBI

BRENDA RALPH LEWIS

MASON CREST PUBLISHERS
www.masoncrest.com

Mason Crest Publishers Inc.
370 Reed Road
Broomall, PA 19008
(866) MCP-BOOK (toll free)
www.masoncrest.com

First printing

1 2 3 4 5 6 7 8 9 10

Library of Congress Cataloging-in-Publication Data on file
at the Library of Congress

ISBN 1-59084-403-3

Editorial and design by
Amber Books Ltd.
Bradley's Close
74–77 White Lion Street
London N1 9PF
www.amberbooks.co.uk

Project Editor: Michael Spilling
Design: Graham Curd
Picture Research: Natasha Jones

Printed and bound in Jordan

Picture credits
Federal Emergency Management Agency: 25 (top); Mary Evans Picture Library: 10, 13;
Popperfoto: 6, 8, 14, 16, 17, 19, 20, 22, 27, 34–35, 36, 39, 40, 42, 43, 44, 45, 46, 48, 50,
54, 55, 60, 65, 66, 68, 74, 79, 82, 84, 87, 88; Topham Picturepoint: 24–25, 26, 29, 72–73,
76, 83, 86. TRH Pictures: 31, 32, 53, 57, 59, 62, 69, 71; U.S. Coast Guard: 75.
Front cover: Popperfoto.

DEDICATION

This book is dedicated to those who perished in the terrorist attacks of
September 11, 2001, and to all the committed individuals who continually
serve to defend freedom and protect the American people.

CONTENTS

INTRODUCTION

September 11, 2001, saw terrorism cast its lethal shadow across the globe. The deaths inflicted at the Twin Towers, at the Pentagon, and in Pennsylvania were truly an attack on the world and civilization itself. However, even as the impact echoed around the world, the forces of decency were fighting back: Americans drew inspiration from a new breed of previously unsung, everyday heroes. Amid the smoking rubble, firefighters, police officers, search-and-rescue, and other "first responders" made history. The sacrifices made that day will never be forgotten.

Out of the horror and destruction, we have fought back on every front. When the terrorists struck, their target was not just the United States, but also the values that the American people share with others all over the world who cherish freedom. Country by country, region by region, state by state, we have strengthened our public-safety efforts to make it much more difficult for terrorists.

Others have come to the forefront: from the Coast Guard to the Border Patrol, a wide range of agencies work day and night for our protection. Before the terrorist attacks of September 11, 2001, launched them into the spotlight, the courage of these guardians went largely unrecognized, although in truth, the sense of service was always honor enough for them. We can never repay the debt we owe them, but by increasing our understanding of the work they do, the *Rescue and Prevention: Defending Our Nation* books will enable us to better appreciate our brave defenders.

Steven L. Labov—CISM, MSO, CERT 3
Chief of Department, United States Search and Rescue Task Force

Left: A German police special forces officer walks past an Air Malta Boeing 737 that was hijacked to Cologne-Bonn Airport in June 1997.

TAKING HOSTAGES, PAST AND PRESENT

To become a hostage is a terrifying experience. One moment, you are leading an ordinary life, uninterrupted by dramatic events; the next, you are the prisoner of a desperado who is using you to make demands. And if these demands are not met, you may be killed. Suddenly, your life has changed and you have no control over it. All you can do is wait and pray.

Now your life is in the hands of two groups of people: those who have taken you hostage and those who are trying to free you. The Federal Bureau of Investigation (FBI) has its own Hostage Rescue Team (HRT), whose members have been specially trained to free hostages unharmed.

The HRT was established in 1983 by Danny O. Coulson, an FBI operative who had spent over 30 years dealing with **terrorists**, assassins, and other criminals. The FBI had scored great successes against criminals, but in cases where hostages had been involved, too many of them had died. It was time, Coulson believed, to form a special organization dedicated to saving the lives of hostages.

Hostage taking is not a new development. The difference is that

Left: Terry Waite, an adviser to Britain's Archbishop of Canterbury, negotiated the release of many hostages in the Middle East before himself becoming a hostage in Beirut, Lebanon. He was set free in 1991, after five years.

today it is much more violent and dangerous than it used to be; this is chiefly because of the modern guns, bombs, and other weapons that can be used in terrorist and hostage situations.

IN ANCIENT TIMES

In the second century B.C. in the Middle East, the Syrians seized the relatives of community leaders as hostages in their fight against their Jewish neighbors. The idea was to make the Jews think twice about attacking the Syrian army: if they did so, then their relatives would be killed.

The army of ancient Rome did the same with the tribes they were fighting and sometimes made hostages of a chieftain's children to make sure he behaved himself. Sometimes, money was the motive for hostage taking. For example, in medieval times, important people like kings or nobles were often held as hostages in exchange for large **ransoms**. This was usually after they had been taken prisoner in a war; but as hostages they were well-treated, with all the honor due to their high position.

ROYAL HOSTAGES

Money and vengeance was the reason behind the most famous piece of hostage taking in English history: King Richard I, known as the Lionheart. In 1191, Richard was one of the leaders of the Third

Left: One of the most famous hostages in history was the English king Richard I, known as "Lionheart," shown here on the Third Crusade to the Holy Land (today's Israel) in 1191.

Crusade against the Muslims in the Holy Land. While in the Holy Land, it seems that Richard insulted another leader, Duke Leopold of Austria. Leopold vowed to get his revenge.

In 1192, Richard was in Vienna, Austria, on his way home to England when Duke Leopold captured him and flung him in prison. The Duke then demanded an enormous ransom of 150,000 marks (around U.S. $67,000) for Richard's release. Richard remained Leopold's prisoner and hostage for over a year, until February 1194—that was how long it took for the government in England to raise the ransom by taxing Richard's subjects.

THE CONQUISTADORS

Almost four centuries later, in central and south America, the Spanish **conquistadors** found themselves facing danger. To protect themselves, they took hostages. The first of the conquistadors was Hernan Cortes, who invaded Aztec Mexico in 1519. By November, Cortes and his small army of only 550 Spaniards had reached Tenochtitlán (now Mexico City). They were greeted enthusiastically by the people of Tenochtitlán and their ruler, Montezuma, but not all Aztecs welcomed the Spanish intruders.

The Aztec priests in particular hated and feared them, believing that the Spaniards meant to destroy the Aztec religion and the Aztec

Right: In 1520, the Spanish conquistador Hernan Cortes took the Aztec ruler Montezuma as hostage in order to control his people. Here, Montezuma greets a crowd of his people to show that he has not been harmed.

WHY TAKE HOSTAGES?

Hostage taking is a form of blackmail. Terrorists kidnap people to use as a bargaining chip in negotiations with governments and other authorities.

The terrorists can make many demands: large amounts of money; an aircraft or other vehicle, so that they can escape arrest; or the release from prison of a criminal connected with the terrorist organization. Whatever they want, the threat is the same: "You agree to our demands, or we will kill our hostages."

It is a very dangerous situation, but it has certain advantages for the terrorists. All extremists and terrorists need and want publicity, so that the cause for which they are fighting becomes known. They know that if they take hostages, this will be widely reported on TV and in newspapers.

Taking hostages brings other benefits as well. It lets terrorists show how powerful they are by making problems for governments and forcing them to spend time, money, and effort to counter them.

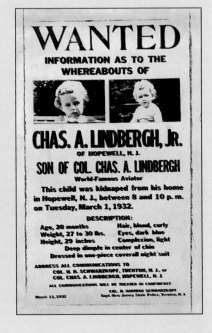

The young son of Charles Lindbergh, the first man to fly solo across the Atlantic, was kidnapped in 1932. Tragically, the child was later found murdered.

empire with it. This is exactly what the Spaniards meant to do, but they were greatly outnumbered; the Aztecs could easily have killed all of them. So, to gain control over the Aztecs, Cortes decided to make Montezuma his hostage. The emperor was imprisoned in his palace and from then on, he was manipulated by Cortes and forced to obey his orders.

The Aztec priests rebelled. Montezuma was killed, and the Spaniards were driven out of Tenochtitlán. However, they returned in 1521 to defeat the Aztecs and take over the Aztec empire.

In 1532, a second Spanish conquistador, Francisco Pizarro, was facing a similar situation in Tahuantinsuyu, the great Inca empire that covered present-day Peru, Bolivia, and Ecuador, as well as parts of Chile. Pizarro's army was even smaller than Cortes'—only 180 men. Soon after he arrived at the Inca town of Cajamarca, Pizarro took as his hostage the Inca ruler, Sapa Inca (Supreme Lord) Atahualpa. Just as Cortes had done 13 years earlier in Mexico, Pizarro was making sure that he and his army would be safe.

Atahualpa had extraordinary power over his Inca subjects: they believed he was a god and obeyed him without question. So, when Atahualpa offered Pizarro a gigantic ransom for his freedom—a room full of gold, and two rooms of silver—the Incas obediently collected these precious metals from all over Tahuantinsuyu. Atahualpa now expected to be released. And Pizarro now realized just powerful his hostage was; the Sapa Inca could order his people to do anything. What if he directed his subjects to kill all Spaniards? Pizarro could not afford to let Atahualpa go. Instead, he executed his hostage in 1533.

Looking exhausted, but relieved that the nightmare was over, hostages taken after a rebel attack on the Japanese ambassador's home in Lima, Peru, walk to freedom in December 1996.

NO NEGOTIATIONS

In the past, kings and rulers like Richard the Lionheart, Montezuma, and Atahualpa, and members of the aristocracy were the only people worth taking hostage. Who else had the money and power to pay big ransoms? Today, hostage taking is a different matter—and a much more dangerous one. Anyone, rich or poor, powerful or ordinary, can become a hostage. The hostage takers gamble that the hostages' governments will agree to any demands they make.

However, this is not always the case. The U.S. and British governments, for example, consistently refuse to negotiate with terrorists and hostage takers. If there are no negotiations, no

French GIGN elite special forces storm the hijacked Air France Airbus on the runway at Marseille in December 1996. Loaded with 172 passengers, the plane was seized by Algerian fundamentalists at Algiers airport.

demands will be met. This, of course, puts the hostages in great danger. The same is true for hostage rescuers. Somehow, they have to free hostages in situations in which the hostage takers are willing to use guns and other weapons to stop them. Sometimes, hostage takers are willing to blow up the sites where the hostages are being kept—whether buildings or aircraft. Sometimes, too, they will even kill themselves rather than let the rescuers succeed.

In short, hostage takers and hostage rescuers have goals that are directly opposite. They struggle against each other to get their own way and win, but they also have quite different views about the value of human life. Every living thing wants to survive, but hostage takers who are willing to kill themselves ignore this natural instinct. For the rescuers, on the other hand, the survival of the hostages always comes first.

This is why the task of hostage rescue is so difficult as well as dangerous. It is not enough for rescuers to have more or better weapons or more men and women than their opponents. They need patience, careful planning, and a great deal of courage to make sure that the hostage takers are defeated and that the hostages themselves survive. The hostage takers, on the other hand, are far more desparate and have much less to lose.

Right: At Waco, Texas, where the extremist Branch Davidian sect was under siege in 1993, the FBI used helicopter gunships to attack the compound. A gun battle and fire ensued in which the leader, David Koresh, and 75 of his followers died. The FBI believed that Koresh was holding women and children hostage.

RESCUE AT ENTEBBE

The Israeli raid on Entebbe, Uganda, is widely recognized as the model of how to rescue hostages and defeat the plans of terrorist hostage takers.

On June 27, 1976, Air France Flight 139, from Athens, Greece, to Tel Aviv, Israel, was hijacked by seven terrorists in the name of the Palestine Liberation Organization (PLO). On board were 207 passengers. The pilot was ordered to fly to Uganda, whose ruler, Idi

The 103 hostages who survived received a tremendous welcome when they arrived at Ben Gurion Airport in Tel Aviv.

Amin, supported the PLO. The aircraft landed at Entebbe, near Lake Victoria. First, the terrorists separated the passengers. One hundred and six were either Israelis or Jews, and these people were put into the airport's Old Terminal building. The other 101, people of other nationalities, were released. Finally, the terrorists issued their demand: the release of 53 terrorists from prison. If this demand were not met, they would kill the passengers.

The families of the passengers wanted the Israeli government to agree to the terrorists' demands. It refused. Instead, it decided on a daring plan to rescue the hostages. Operation Thunderbolt was launched. First, the Israelis announced that they would negotiate with the terrorists at Entebbe. Previously, they had always refused to do this. Secretly, however, the Israelis prepared four large Hercules C130 transport aircraft to fly the rescuers to Entebbe, which lay 2,500 miles (4,025 km) away.

The Hercules aircraft landed at the airport at 11:01 P.M. on July 4, 1976. The Israelis went into action at once. First, they killed the Ugandan soldiers guarding the hostages. Next, they shouted to the hostages to lie flat on the floor. A fierce gun battle with the PLO followed. It lasted only three minutes. All seven terrorists were killed. The Israelis ordered the hostages onto the Hercules transports, and at 12:02 A.M. on July 5, just an hour after landing at Entebbe, the aircraft took off and flew the 2,500 miles back to Israel. Sadly, the Israeli commander, Colonel Jonathan Netanyahu, was killed in the last moments of the rescue.

LEARNING TO BE A HOSTAGE RESCUER

When he first began considering what sort of men and women would make good agents for the FBI's Hostage Rescue Team, Danny Coulson knew straightaway the kind of people he was looking for—extraordinary people.

HRT agents must be able to act on their own, but also know how to work with other agents. There will be exciting jobs and dull jobs, but both kinds have to be done in the same way—well and thoroughly. Agents cannot be afraid to take risks, but at the same time, they cannot be hotheads craving excitement. A sense of humor is particularly important. Humor helps break tensions and keeps agents from getting uptight about the job. It also helps to calm nerves and bind the team together—and the team is the most important thing of all.

TOUGH TRAINING

The first HRT **trainees** were a group of 50 men and one woman. Arriving at the training academy at Quantico, Virginia, they were also the first to discover that working for the HRT is very, very tough. For a start, they soon realized that agents must have strong hands, arms, and backs. To reach the sorts of places where their

Left: A U.S. Navy SEAL rescuer landing by parachute at a training demonstration, accompanied by the "Stars and Stripes."

terrorist opponents might be holed up, agents may have to make great physical efforts—jumping, climbing, swimming, running, crawling, parachuting, or **abseiling** down ropes from helicopters.

However, just managing this is not enough; trainees must also arrive at the "battleground" ready and fit to fight their opponents. The first test is a 4-mile (6-km) run. Next, they climb 20-foot (6-m) ropes over and over again, and afterward do several push-ups and pull-ups in the academy's gym. If these hard exercises are a struggle for a trainee—no good. If they manage to complete the exercises,

but become exhausted—also no good.

The ability to obey orders instantly and without question is also tested in the gym. To tell which of the first trainees had this ability, Coulson watched their faces as they received instructions from the physical trainer.

FBI agents doing some tough physical training at their base in Quantico, Virginia.

If they looked as if they could not wait to get going and showed no fear or doubt—good. If they frowned or looked worried—no good.

Then comes training in the use of guns. All trainees are given .375 Magnum revolvers, but not to shoot at stationary targets. They must use their guns in training in the same way they will have to use them in a real situation, with terrorists shooting back at them. This means firing guns accurately while running.

In later training for full-scale antiterrorist missions, they use live

Hostage rescuers have to be accurate shots and must be ready to exchange fire with hostage-takers and terrorists. Here, agents do shooting practice with pump-action shotguns at Quantico, Virginia.

WHO DARES, WINS: BRITAIN'S SPECIAL AIR SERVICE

On April 30, 1980, six Arab terrorists forced their way into the Embassy of Iran in London, England. They took 26 hostages. Their demand was simple: their own independent state in southwest Iran in return for the hostages' lives. In the next six days, five hostages were

During the siege of the Iranian Embassy in 1980, the hostages and their captors were provided with food by the police. Here, one of the hostage takers comes out of the building to collect a meal.

released, another was executed, and two others were injured.

Television cameras were filming outside the embassy building when, suddenly, viewers heard a loud explosion from bomb charges placed against the windows. Next, eight soldiers abseiled down ropes from the roof and crashed through the windows. In the fight that followed, all but one of the terrorists were killed. The remaining 20 hostages were rescued. The rescuers belonged to a special group—the Special Air Services (SAS), whose motto is "Who Dares, Wins." The SAS are experts at moving silently, hiding where no one can see them, and taking their enemies by surprise.

ammunition. Some of the trainees act as hostages and are placed close to targets representing their terrorist captors. The trick is to shoot down the targets without harming the hostages. It is a test both for these hostages and for the men and women shooting the guns: they are, after all, shooting live bullets close to their friends and teammates.

Training also includes testing whether trainees suffer from **aquaphobia**—fear of water. The reason is simple: in action, agents might have to swim a river or rescue hostages from a boat. The test is designed to be as frightening as possible. A brick is thrown into a swimming pool. The trainees are blindfolded, then told to hold their noses and jump into the pool from a 15-foot (5-m) diving platform. Once in the water, they are not supposed to come to the surface to breathe, but have to stay under and find the brick.

HRT trainees can also not afford to suffer from **acrophobia**—a fear of heights. HRT agents might have to work at great heights, so their training includes a "confidence course" to test whether this might be a problem. This involves using a ladder to climb up five-story buildings. This ladder is unsteady and feels unsafe as it shakes and rolls. Before they start, the trainees are told that if they fall off, they will probably be killed. They are given the choice not to climb it, but if they fail to climb, that is the end of their chance to be chosen for the Hostage Rescue Team.

Right: FBI agents have to be very fit for hostage-rescue work. This picture shows FBI trainees traversing an assault course at their headquarters in Quantico, Virginia.

HRT WEAPONS AND EQUIPMENT

The HRT uses the most up-to-date weapons and equipment in their vital work of saving the lives of hostages. These include:

- Submachine guns: small, rapid-firing weapons
- Handguns: guns that can be fired using only one hand
- Rifles: guns fitted with sights and used by HRT snipers, who shoot from well-hidden places at single targets
- Machine pistols: small handguns that can be fired automatically
- Munitions: explosives that can blow open doors
- Chemical munitions: usually "tear gas," fired in containers from shotguns or launchers to disable terrorists; agents also wear gas masks so that they will not be affected by gas used by terrorists
- Sound and light devices: these produce a loud noise and bright flashes of light, which deafen and confuse terrorists
- Night-vision devices: night-vision goggles or attachments to guns, which have their own infrared illuminators that enable agents to see in the dark
- Body armor: a vest made of Kevlar or other material that can resist bullets
- Tools for entering buildings: a ram, to batter at the door; pry bar, to open doors at the side; sledge hammer, for breaking down obstacles; and bolt cutter, to cut through bolts and locks on doors
- Microphones: small listening devices that enable agents to hear what's going on inside a building
- Video systems: small viewing devices that enable agents to see what's going on inside a building.

Pictures of terrorists—both men and women—pointing guns are used in hostage-rescue training to enable FBI agents to return fire quickly and accurately.

FBI agents in training, landing from a helicopter on top of a building. This building was specially built of plywood for the exercise.

OBSTACLES AND EXAMINATIONS

FBI trainees lose the chance to become HRT officers if they fail to pass the FBI's extremely tough **obstacle course**. This is similar to the U.S. Marine Corps' course, but has obstacles up to 6 inches (15 cm) higher. The FBI course begins with a huge leap up into the air to grab a parallel bar and get over it, and includes carrying another trainee over a distance of 60 yards (66 m)—rescue for the HRT does not mean rescuing hostages only, but also carrying injured teammates out of danger.

There are also examinations to pass. One of these involves being ordered out of bed in the middle of the night to watch a video showing a real-life fight against terrorists. They then have to write a report about it, the sort of report that would be written by an FBI agent. The idea of this examination is to test the trainees' **powers of observation** under difficult circumstances, when they are only half awake—how well did they observe the events on the video and how clearly did they remember it afterward?

HRT agents must be able to observe and notice small signs or changes in the way terrorists operate. To combat the hostage takers, they must know and understand the enemy. This could prevent agents from being taken by surprise by their opponents and help them improve their chances of rescuing hostages without suffering casualties themselves.

In 1983, the first year of the Hostage Rescue Team, a total of 150 trainees went through what must be the toughest set of tests ever created. Only 50 of them, the very best in the group, were chosen to be members of the Team.

THE LAST FIGHT

The last part of a rescue operation often takes place in rooms where the hostages are being held. This is the most dangerous situation, with hostages, their captors, and their rescuers all together in a small space. So rescuers train hard to make sure that they get it right.

Four rescuers, sometimes five, do the work of "clearing the room"—killing or capturing the hostage takers and rescuing the hostages.

- The point man goes in first, holding in one hand a mirror or other device to enable him to see if anyone is hiding round a corner; and in the other, a handgun to shoot the first hostage taker to threaten him.
- The first clearing man follows the point man and is armed with a submachine gun. He shoots at other hostage takers in the room.
- The team leader deals with any hostage takers still able to fight. Once the team leader is in control, the point man and clearing man can leave and move on to the next room.
- The second clearing man shoots off any locks or door hinges preventing the rescuers from reaching the hostage takers. He also supports the team leader in dealing with the hostage takers.
- The rear guard may use a ram to break down a door, and guards the rest of the rescue team as they clear the room.

These heavily armed hostage-rescue agents wear protective gas masks to prevent them from being affected if tear gas has to be used against hostage takers.

PREPARING TO RESCUE HOSTAGES

You might not think so from the action movies you see, but rescuing hostages does not necessarily involve barging into buildings, firing guns, crashing cars, or making a lot of noise. In fact, hostage rescue is often a quiet and calm affair. What is needed is patience, because a lot of time can pass before the action itself begins; this waiting can even be a bit boring.

GATHERING INFORMATION

Before a rescue can begin, there is a lot the agents need to know, both about the hostages and their captors: how many people are involved; what weapons are being used; and the site where they are holed up, including the layout and the best way to enter. Rescuers even have to know what the hostages are wearing, just in case the hostage takers exchange clothes with them. When the guns start firing, the rescuers do not want to find that they have hurt the wrong people.

Rescuers also have to survey the surroundings of the site where the hostages are held. The most helpful

Left: Brazilian Special Forces Police taking up positions outside a Sao Paolo mansion where its owner, Silvio Santos, was being held hostage in August 2001. Santos' captor eventually surrendered.

places for them are high ground or hills. This will give the rescuers better chances of observing the building. High ground is also a good hiding place for **snipers**. Specially trained to shoot quickly and accurately, snipers have the ability to shoot a hostage taker who has come out into the open accompanied by a hostage without harming the hostage.

Close to some houses and buildings will be **gulleys** or **culverts**. These are useful for hiding rescuers as they approach the building and let them come nearer than would be possible if the ground were flat and level. However, this advantage may also be apparent to the hostage takers themselves: gulleys and culverts also make good escape routes. The team must ensure that the hostage takers do not have the opportunity to leave the area with their hostages.

In any hostage-rescue situation, it is impossible to guarantee that no mistakes will be made. However, the more information the rescuers have, the better their chances of success. This information can come from various sources. Police or FBI records will show if the hostage takers have committed crimes in the past, particularly violent crimes. Do they have a history of drug taking or mental illness? The records of hospitals and clinics may provide clues. How old are they? If the hostage takers are young, they are more likely to be violent. Have they suffered a personal tragedy—perhaps divorce or a death in their family? If so, the hostage taking or other crimes of violence may occur on the anniversaries of such events.

Rescuers who have **staked out** a building with hostages inside can also tell a great deal simply by using a pair of binoculars. Hostage takers do not usually remain hidden inside a building for

Belgian hostage rescuers, including sharpshooters, surround a house in the town of Grace-Hollogne, where a woman was taken hostage in January 2000. She was eventually rescued unharmed.

the whole time. To ensure that everyone is aware of the situation and of what they are demanding, they will appear with their hostages at windows or even at the door. The rescuers watching from outside can decide just how likely they are to be violent—do the hostage takers keep on making threats, holding a gun to a hostage's head and talking about killing him or her?

ELECTRONIC DEVICES

More important information can be gained by using high-tech electronic devices. Many of these cannot be used from a distance, so

These hostage rescuers used special night-vision goggles during an antirebel military action in the Philippines in 2002. Members of a rebel Muslim group, Abu Sayyaf, took two Americans hostage for more than eight months before their release was secured.

rescuers must risk approaching the building to attach the devices to the walls, ventilation systems, or even the chimneys on the roof. Of course, all this must be done quietly and carefully to prevent the hostage takers from realizing what is happening.

A device often used is the **endoscope**—in effect, this is a TV on a tube that can be pushed through holes in walls. The rescuers are then able to watch the hostage takers inside. Microphones in the chimney can pick up what is being said, as can electronic **stethoscopes**, which are similar to the stethoscopes used by doctors to hear what is happening inside the body.

It is even possible for the rescuers to learn how the hostage takers are thinking. Do they keep on talking about dying? Do they sound or look as if they are nervous? Do they boast about how powerful they are or how many booby traps they have laid around the building? Do they threaten to kill any rescuer who dares come too near? If the answer to these questions is yes, the rescuers know that the hostage takers are desperate, possibly suicidal, and certainly unpredictable. They may turn violent at any time, without warning, and kill their hostages and also, perhaps, themselves.

THE NEGOTIATORS

All this information helps build up a picture of the type of people the rescuers are dealing with and how they should be approached. This is where the hostage-rescue negotiator comes in. Negotiating a way out of a hostage situation is a tricky business. The hostage takers must not be made angry or upset during negotiations. They must not feel that negotiators are bullying or criticizing them.

Negotiators try to make them believe that they understand, and even sympathize with, whatever pressures have driven them to take hostages in the first place. So negotiators speak very calmly. If they are visible to the hostage takers, they must not make any suspicious

In June 2000, Argentine news photographer Martin Firpo was threatened by an armed robber inside a gas station near Buenos Aires. Police later seized the robber and rescued Firpo.

Negotiations taking place at the Olympic village in Munich, Germany in 1972, where nine Israeli athletes were held hostage by Palestinian terrorists. Unfortunately, all the hostages died.

movements—as if they are reaching for a gun, for instance. None of this, however, means that hostage takers are able to start thinking that they can have whatever they want: the negotiator must always be in control of the situation.

One way of achieving this is to keep the hostage takers talking, forcing them to concentrate on small, unimportant details. Suppose

HOW NOT TO RESCUE HOSTAGES

• May 14, 1974: Three Palestinian terrorists attacked a school in Ma'Alot, Israel, and took 100 students as hostages. Unfortunately, the hostage rescuers, an antiterrorist unit called Sayeret Mat'kal, did not have the right information about where the hostage takers were in the school building and they waited too long to attack. As a result, 26 of the hostages were killed and another 60 badly injured.

• November 25, 1985: Egyptian hostage-rescue commandos, Force 777, made a disastrous attack on an Egypt Air plane that had been hijacked on the way from Athens, Greece, to the island of Malta. Everything went wrong. Force 777 used explosives to enter the plane, and once inside, they opened fire indescriminately.
In all, 57 passengers died.

Hostage rescuers have to be well protected for their risky work, not only with guns, but also with shields and protective helmets.

the hostage takers want a supply of coffee. The negotiator will prolong the conversation by asking what kind of coffee? Instant? Filter? Cappuccino? Espresso? With milk or without milk? With sugar or without sugar…and so on. The hostage takers may not care what kind of coffee they get, but by being made to talk about such trivial matters, they cannot be doing anything else in the meantime. And as long as the conversation continues, they cannot be thinking quite so much about their hostages.

Two American missionaries who became hostages in the Philippines had their picture taken while in captivity in 2002, backed by their heavily masked captors.

Hostages captured at the Myanmar Embassy in Bangkok, Thailand, in 1999, celebrate their release.

KNOW YOUR ENEMY

Negotiators might also grant small concessions, perhaps agreeing to let food into the building. However, in exchange, they will want one or more hostages set free. If the hostage takers are hungry enough, they may agree, especially if they have several hostages and thus can spare a few without weakening their own position. This way, the HRT can reduce the number of hostages at risk.

If the electricity or water supplies have been turned off from outside the building, this can make things uncomfortable for everyone inside. Negotiators may be willing to restore these supplies—but only if more hostages are set free or their captors agree to let them talk to their worried relatives outside. Negotiators will not agree to any big demands, such as sending alcohol, drugs, or weapons into the building; any or all of these could make the situation much worse.

Whatever small concessions the negotiator makes, the basic situation remains the same. Most of the hostages and their captors are still holed up inside the building, and the rescuers are still surrounding it. But while the negotiator keeps the hostage takers occupied, the rescuers are waiting for the right moment to enter the house, rescue the hostages, and kill their captors or take them prisoner.

Of course, not all hostage-rescue plans go as smoothly as this, and sometimes rescuers have to use force to resolve the situation. Even so, the lives of many hostages have been saved by careful, patient rescue methods, and many hostage takers have been prevented from achieving their demands.

THE SNIPERS

For most people, the sharpshooting sniper belongs to wars, killing enemies by shooting from hidden places and never missing their targets. It is true that in war snipers are the secret, silent killers, hidden away in trees or on high ground, behind bushes or walls. But snipers are also used in rescuing hostages, and may sometimes kill hostage takers—and this is not their only role.

Because they are hidden, snipers can provide valuable information about the place where hostages are being held. They may be the first to realize that hostage takers are attempting an escape or see where they have placed dangerous booby traps. The rest of the rescue team may not be able to see where an armed hostage taker is lying in wait for them—but the snipers can, and are able to provide warning.

Hostage situations tend to take place in towns or other areas crowded with ordinary people. One of the sniper's tasks is to protect the hostages and also other members of the rescue team. When the rest of the team prepares to enter a building from one side, snipers will often fire their guns at the opposite side. This is known as creating a **diversion**. Hostage takers, hearing bullets whack against

Left: A sniper in position, gun at the ready, under the shadow of a large bell. This offers the marksman a superb vantage point from which to observe a hostage situation and, if necessary, shoot the hostage takers.

the outside wall, are made to think that the attack is coming from over there.

On those occasions when a sniper has to kill, it is usually because the hostages or the rescue team are in danger. For example, a hostage taker may force a hostage to walk in front, as a shield against being attacked. What the sniper must do is wait for a chance to shoot the hostage taker, but not the hostage.

WHO ARE THE SNIPERS?

Snipers are very special people. First, they have to be physically strong: snipers often have to climb up trees or hills to get into place at the scene of hostage taking. They must also be very patient, because they have to wait for the best chance to hit their targets: more often than not, the best chance comes only after some time. Snipers cannot afford to be nervous, and they must never hesitate. They must always act as soon as they see their opportunity and since this is usually an opportunity to kill, they must do it without thinking twice about it.

CRACK SHOTS

Snipers are often called "crack shots," which means that they are very accurate and know exactly when and where to fire their guns. However, they need more than a firm, steady hand, good eyesight,

Left: SWAT officers outside an arcade in Santa Monica, California, in June 2000, wait for the right moment to deal with two gunmen who have taken 15 hostages inside the building.

and the best telescopic sights for their rifles. Hostage rescues can take place in all sorts of weather conditions—rain, wind, even snow and ice. None of this should make any difference to the sniper's expertise. They must be able to calculate how to shoot accurately even in heavy rain or when the wind is blowing hard. Most often, snipers will have to shoot at moving targets. Hostage takers are not going to stand still or put themselves in a dangerous position, thus making it easier for snipers to get them in their sights. They will probably be on the move all the time.

Snipers also have to be adaptable, able to shoot from various positions. Firing from a rooftop, for instance, is quite different from hiding in a tree or inside a building and firing from there. Because of this, snipers practice using their guns in all the situations that might arise when there are hostages to be rescued.

"TRAFFIC LIGHTS" IN HOSTAGE RESCUE

It is not always possible for the rescue teams to talk to snipers while a hostage rescue is ongoing. For this reason, many of these teams use "traffic light" colors as a code:

- Red light: Do not shoot
- Yellow light: Shoot, but only if it means saving a life; the yellow light tends to be used when no hostages have been killed or injured
- Green light: Shoot as soon as the hostage takers are lined up, in sight; the green light tends to be used when hostage takers have already killed or injured some of their hostages

Hostage rescuers use high-tech equipment, including special radios and televisions, to help them observe and monitor the hostage situation. This way, they can remain in close contact with the negotiators, who may give them the instruction to open fire.

In addition, snipers have to be able to think and act quickly. Sometimes, there will be no time to make careful preparations. In such cases, they must select their targets, work out the range or distance between themselves and the target, and know instantly what ammunition they must use—all in a few seconds. If snipers cannot work this fast, the chance to stop or kill a hostage taker and rescue a hostage may be lost.

The first thing to do is to become familiar with the area they have to cover and make sure they know its features—trees, hills, telegraph poles, even mail boxes. Snipers cannot afford to overlook even the smallest detail. Anything and everything can be important. Before snipers can get into the right position, they have to do a lot of homework. Using binoculars or the scope on their rifles, which makes their targets look bigger, they must make a thorough reconnaissance of the area where the hostages are being held and of the surrounding areas.

These children at a French nursery school were taken hostage in 1993, but were rescued by the police. Here, policemen comfort the children after their ordeal.

These strange-looking creatures are not aliens from another world—they are sharpshooting snipers in disguise outside the German Central Bank in Aachen, where three people were taken hostage in December 1999. Effective camouflage is an essential part of the sniper's equipment.

THE SNIPER'S HIDE

The place where snipers conceal themselves is known as a "hide." In a town or city, the best hide is usually inside an office or an apartment, preferably in a high-rise block on the opposite side of a

THE IMPORTANCE OF CAMOUFLAGE

Another important skill for snipers is an understanding of camouflage. Camouflage comes from the French "camoufler," meaning "to disguise." If snipers take up position high in a tree, for example, they must disguise themselves so that they become part of that tree. By hanging twigs and leaves on clothing or helmets, or wearing clothes that have wavy green and brown patterns, the snipers will blend in with their surroundings. Other hostage rescuers use camouflage, of course, but it is especially important for snipers.

street to the building where a hostage incident has occurred. The snipers can then choose which floor gives them best the advantage; if possible, they will choose a higher position, which lets them look down on the hostage takers and their hostages.

Buildings like these also offer snipers a lot of protection. It is likely to have many windows; all will be opened so that the hostage taker cannot guess which window the sniper is using. Snipers will also conceal themselves behind the curtains at a window.

Window frames and windowsills in city buildings can, of course, be dusty. When snipers fire their guns, the dust can be disturbed. This gives them away and may also interfere with the telescopic sights on their guns. To prevent this from happening, a damp cloth is often placed under the muzzle of a sniper's gun.

Roofs make less-than-satisfactory hides for snipers. For a start, they are out in the open, at the mercy of the weather. Second,

Among this mass of leaves and foliage, a heavily camouflaged sniper is hiding. Only the tip of his gun-barrel is visible.

snipers dare not raise their heads or their shoulders too high above the roof, because then they can be seen, silhouetted against the sky. On a roof, snipers always have to fire downward, at an angle, and this may not help them to be absolutely accurate with their shots.

There is a way around these problems, however. Many roofs have "boxes" that contain the ducts for air conditioning or central heating. Snipers may, therefore, make their own box out of cardboard, painting it to look like the other rooftop boxes.

THE ART OF RECONNAISSANCE

"Reconnaissance" comes from the Old French word, "reconnoistre," which means "to recognize." Reconnaissance will also reveal whether there are any obstacles, like gates or small buildings, which might interfere with their line of fire. Snipers may not be able to avoid these obstacles altogether, but they can at least take this into consideration when choosing their position.

Reconnaissance is important, too, in helping to spot a position that is closest to the target. Of course, events do not always go according to plan, so snipers will be careful to choose two or three positions. In some situations, the sniper may use any or all of the chosen positions.

Suppose a sniper is seen by the hostage takers during the course of negotiations. They could take advantage of this by demanding that the sniper be removed. The negotiator agrees, the sniper moves, and

Right: This sniper is in a good position—well hidden behind a fence with plenty of shade to mask his movements.

Policemen in Luxembourg take up position on a roof overlooking a day care center where children were held hostage by a man armed with a knife, a gun, and a grenade in 2000.

the hostage takers think they have scored a victory. But what has actually happened is that the sniper has simply moved to another place, and the hostage takers are still within range of his rifle. The snipers may themselves choose to move, particularly if a shot has been fired, thus giving away their position. Staying where they are might mean risking death or injury if the hostage takers decide to open fire on this known position.

Snipers often work with observers, who provide important backup. Observers help in reconnoitring the area. If a stakeout continues for a long time, observers will give the snipers a rest by taking over their rifles for a while. At other times, while the sniper is occupied, their observers are free to communicate with the rest of the rescue team and let them know the situation. The observer also has the job of defending the sniper's position, if necessary, and making sure that the position is safe and secure.

KEEPING A RECORD

It may also be the job of the observer to log, or record, a hostage-taking incident. A log has at least two important purposes. First of all, what happens in one incident, including what action the snipers take, can provide valuable information for use in other hostage situations. Second, after an incident is over, there may be an official enquiry; the observer's log will provide evidence for that enquiry.

The log may also be used as evidence if hostage takers are captured and are later put on trial. Anyone who takes hostages always attracts a lot of anger from ordinary people, especially when young children have been made hostages. The terror of it is always much worse for these youngsters, who cannot understand what is happening, but know that whatever it is, it is dangerous.

However, a court of law can never afford to be guided by anger or disgust or any other emotion. What counts in a court of law is the evidence, and only the evidence. The log kept at hostage rescue incidents provides some of the evidence that can prove whether hostage takers on trial are guilty or not guilty. Without it, there can be no trial. The hostage takers may walk free, perhaps to take more hostages and frighten more innocent people in the future.

SHIPS AT SEA

A ship at sea is like a world on its own. With its own stores of food and supplies, it can move anywhere across the Earth's seas and oceans. If terrorists attempt to hijack a ship at sea, it is likely that they will make the passengers and crew their hostages.

Moreover, it is likely to be some time before the rescue teams can reach the scene. This leaves the terrorists free to secure the ship and assert their control, robbing the passengers, perhaps even killing some.

If the hijacked ship is a cruise liner, there are usually hundreds of passengers on board who will become hostages for the terrorists. By contrast, a trading ship or oil tanker, with only the crews on board, will mean fewer hostages. Even so, there are serious dangers. An oil tanker damaged in a terrorist attack might leak oil into the sea; or the hostage takers may deliberately leak the oil, using the threat of pollution to reinforce their demands. The marine life in the nearby waters can be poisoned and killed, while the beaches and shorelines and the birds who live on them can be covered in a sticky black mess as the oil drifts in—and birds covered in oil die very easily. Either way, the environmental damage may be considerable.

Left: This well-armed U.S. Navy SEAL is taking part in a training exercise in boarding a ship.

GATHERING INFORMATION

Whatever type of ship is hijacked at sea, the rescuers must first gather as much information about it as possible. The shipping company that owns the ship can answer several important questions. How high up are the decks? Where are the stairways and the passageways or corridors? What sort of lighting system does the ship have? Does the ship have any ladders or ropes along the side of the hull? (These could help the rescuers climb on board.) Do the hatches and portholes open inward or outward, and where are they located? How thick are the windows, and what type of glass are they made of? (The rescuers may have to smash the glass, and they need to know how easy or difficult this is likely to be.)

Once they have boarded a hijacked ship, the rescuers will probably have to break down parts of the **bulkheads**, the partitions between various sections inside. What are these bulkheads made of—steel, aluminum, or some other material? This will determine the type of equipment the rescuers use.

Getting a rescue team onto a hijacked ship—known as **insertion**—can be difficult, regardless if the ship is "under way" (moving over the sea) or "riding at anchor" (stationary). Rescuers climbing up the ship's side from below are at risk from terrorists above them on the deck. Firing guns downward is much easier than firing upward, particularly when hanging on a rope or ladder with

Right: Rescuers assaulting a hostage ship find it safer to approach it from the stern. The hostage takers are less likely to be watching and it is easier to gain access to the decks.

These rigid-hull inflatable boats, which can be blown up with air when needed, were used by the U.S. Navy to pick up SEAL team members in the Arabian Sea in 2001. They are small, fast, and quick to launch, making them ideal for putting hostage-rescue teams onto ships at sea at short notice.

only one hand free for defense. The goal, then, is to insert the team without the terrorists realizing until too late.

Usually, rescuers choose the **stern** of the ship as the place to board. Their intention is to surprise the terrorists by acting as quickly and as silently as possible. There are one or two tricks that can help. The small, fast boat carrying the rescue team can appear to have fishermen on board. These are, of course, rescuers in disguise, but the terrorists are not to know that and are unlikely to think that these "fishermen" are any danger. After all, fishing boats are a common sight at sea—sometimes quite far out to sea, in fact.

THE TOOLS OF HOSTAGE RESCUE

Teams rescuing hostages and dealing with terrorists on board a hijacked ship need special equipment. This includes:

• Buoyancy panels: The SEAL units of the U.S. Navy wear special vests with buoyancy panels that enable the heavy weapons and equipment they carry to "float" in the water.

• Ladders: These are padded so that they do not make a noise when placed against the sides of the ship.

• Carrying weapons: Rescuers climbing on board a ship need both hands free, so they carry their guns and other weapons in slings.

• Night vision: At night, it is particularly dark at sea, especially if the electricity system on a ship has been cut off; the answer to this problem is night-vision equipment. One piece of equipment is a pair of goggles with its own infrared illuminating system; another is night-vision equipment mounted on a rifle. These night-vision optics, as they are called, make the greatest possible use of low light, like starlight or the light of the moon, and enable rescuers to see in the dark.

This is not for real, but it could be! This hostage "victim" is being winched up to a rescue helicopter during an exercise in China in 2001. Hostage-rescue teams need to practice to maintain readiness.

The bogus fishermen may wave, shout, ask for help, perhaps give warnings of approaching storms—anything and everything that can distract or catch the terrorists' attention and prevent them from knowing the ship is being boarded.

FAKE HOLIDAYMAKERS

Another way of distracting the terrorists is for members of the rescue team to pretend they are passengers taking a day trip out at

SWIMMERS IN RESCUE WORK

The swimmers and divers in a hostage rescue team do not usually take part in assaults on hijacked ships. Even so, their role is important. Moving silently and unseen through the water around the ship, swimmers and divers can gather information about the ship and take pictures of it with underwater video and other cameras.

Divers have to be careful not to give themselves away, so they use special breathing apparatus that does not let bubbles rise to the surface while they are underwater. It takes a lot of courage to be a diver in hostage rescue work. The French counterterrorist unit, *Groupe d'Intervention Gendarmerie Nationale* (GIGN), tests its divers with a frightening ordeal. They must dive into the River Seine, which runs through Paris, and lie on the bottom for long periods of time.

These U.S. Navy SEAL frogmen are practicing diving techniques in preparation for potential hostage-rescue situations.

sea from a holiday resort on a nearby coast. They will dress in beach clothes to look perfectly harmless. Some of the girls among the "holidaymakers" have a special trick they can play. They dress up in skimpy bikinis in order to attract the attention of the hostage takers. And while they are eyeing the girls and flirting with them, they are not thinking about anything else. This gives the rescuers a good chance of getting on board the hijacked ship without being noticed. This gives them the advantage of surprise. By the time the hostage takers realize the deception, they are under attack.

USING HELICOPTERS

Rescuers can also be dropped by helicopter. However, this is a noisier way of doing it that will attract a lot of attention. To make sure they do not give the game away too soon, the helicopters approach the ship flying very low over the sea. At the right moment, the helicopter pilot then pulls back on the controls and the helicopter rises up into the sky, over the stern.

Suddenly, rescuers are abseiling fast down ropes, out of the helicopter and directly onto the deck. Before they reach the deck, they may be easy targets for the terrorists, who can pick them off with gunfire. However, the helicopter can give them some protection with covering fire aimed down at the terrorists.

Right: These U.S. Navy SEALs train in onboard-assault techniques. Once it has been decided to rescue hostages using force, the HRT will need to move quickly to neutralize the hostage-takers before any harm comes to the hostages.

THE HIJACK OF THE *ACHILLE LAURO*

Not all hostage-taking incidents end with the death or punishment of the terrorists involved. One such incident was the hijacking of the Italian cruise liner, the *Achille Lauro*, on October 7, 1985.

The liner was sailing along the Egyptian coast from Alexandria to Port Said when it was hijacked by five terrorists of the Palestine Liberation Front (PLF). There were 454 passengers and crew on board. The terrorists demanded that 50 PLF men held prisoner in Israel be freed, or the ship would be blown up. One of the 19 American passengers, a disabled man called

The ill-fated cruise liner *Achille Lauro*, where 454 passengers were held hostage in 1985.

Leon Klinghoffer, argued with the terrorists. They killed him and threw his body overboard, still strapped to his wheelchair.

This produced shock and outrage worldwide, but particularly in the United States. Within a few hours, commandos of the U.S. Navy SEALs arrived at Akrotiri on the Mediterranean island of Cyprus and made preparations to rescue the hostages. However, by the time they were ready, on October 9, the terrorists were no longer on board the ship. They had sailed the *Achille Lauro* to Port Said, where they made new demands. They would surrender, they said, if they were not prosecuted and were released into PLF custody.

The Egyptian government agreed and sent an aircraft to Port Said to fly the terrorists to safety in Tunisia, North Africa. The U.S. government was furious and tried to stop their escape. Two U.S. Navy fighters were sent to force the Egyptian plane to land in Sicily, an island off the southwest coast of Italy.

In Sicily, the terrorists were arrested by the carabinieri, the Italian police. Later, the Italian government let two of them and their leader, Mohamed Abbas, go free. The other two were put on trial and sent to prison.

The rescue team's best defense, however, is speed. The U.S. Navy's counterterrorist unit, SEAL Team 6, is expert in the use of helicopters in rescue work. With helicopters hovering 60 feet (18 m) above the ship, it can land six men down fast ropes within four seconds, even though the deck may be moving up and down with the motion of the sea. Speed is also important for the safety of the helicopter itself. To guard against being shot down, the pilot flies away quickly once the rescue team is safely on board.

French Prime Minister Lionel Jospin (center) is shown a grenade launcher used by the GIGN antiterrorist squad in 1999. The GIGN are famous for their counterterrorist and hostage-rescue capabilities.

These two fast U.S. Coast Guard pursuit boats can be used for pursuing hijacked ships and boats.

Now that the rescuers are on board, they must move fast to find the hostages. This is no easy task. The inside of a ship is a mass of stairways, passages, and cabins. All of them have to be searched, and any of them may contain one or more terrorists willing to fight to the death. Some of the passageways are very narrow, so the rescuers have to bend low, or even crawl along the floor.

As always, the first thing to be done is to get the hostages to a place of safety elsewhere on the ship. As for the terrorists, the ship they hijacked is now a trap, with few ways of escaping. Sometimes, it is possible for them to negotiate for their freedom. But in most situations, there is nowhere to go. Either they surrender or they are killed by the security forces.

HOSTAGES ON AIRCRAFT

In 1968, defeating terrorists and rescuing hostages gained a new urgency. On July 23 of that year, a Boeing 707 airliner belonging to El Al, the Israeli national airline, was hijacked by three members of the Popular Front for the Liberation of Palestine (PFLP).

The 32 passengers on board became hostages. The airliner was scheduled to fly from Tel Aviv, Israel, to Rome, Italy. However, the pilot was forced to fly to Algiers, Algeria. Once there, the hijackers refused to release their hostages until they were guaranteed that they would not be punished or imprisoned for their crime. After five weeks, all the hostages were released, and the hijackers escaped. The incident made front-page news around the world. However, it was not the first time an aircraft had been hijacked. The first known airliner hijacking occurred in Peru. On February 21, 1931, an American pilot, Byron Rickards, was taken hostage, then held for 10 days by revolutionaries who wanted to use his aircraft for transport.

After World War II ended, several planes were hijacked by refugees whose lives were in danger because they were opposed to the new governments, usually Communist governments, that had

Left: Here, U.S. airport security men watch as a Boeing 757 takes off from Los Angeles International Airport. Since the terrorist outrages of September 11, 2001, airport security throughout the United States has been greatly increased.

come to power in their countries. Hijacking a plane and getting it to fly where they wanted was their way of escaping.

AIR PIRACY

What made the El Al incident of 1968 different was not the hijacking itself, but the fact that it was done for political reasons. The PFLP, which had been formed only seven months earlier, wanted to publicize their quarrel with Israel over the treatment of Palestinian Arabs. The PFLP and its activities have been known worldwide ever since.

This was the first of many PFLP hijackings. Even worse, it was also the start of an enormous increase in this type of crime, which became known as air piracy. In 1969, there were 82 aircraft hijackings, more than twice the number that had occurred in the previous 20 years. Between 1967 and 1976, some 385 aircraft were hijacked. Over the next 10 years, the situation seemed to improve. Hijackings dropped to 300, and between 1987 and 1996, they dropped even lower, to 212.

Even so, this meant that hundreds of passengers and crew were still becoming hostages. This represented a new international problem: any country's aircraft could be hijacked at any time, anywhere in the world.

SPECIAL DANGERS

El Al, the Israeli airline, was in a particularly dangerous position, since the quarrel with the Palestinians continued for many years—and is still not at an end. El Al aircraft often carried Jewish passen-

This hijacker, his identity kept hidden by his hood, was one of the terrorists who took several Americans hostage at Beirut Airport, in Lebanon, in 1985. The hostages were eventually released unharmed.

gers visiting Israel, or Israeli citizens returning home from abroad. El Al, therefore, continued to be a target for terrorists. Because of this, El Al is allowed even today to park its aircraft in special areas at airports around the world. These areas are well away from any place where a terrorist might be able to approach and get on board. No other airline has felt the need to take such precautions, but all have increased their security. Before passengers are allowed to board aircraft, they are now searched for weapons. They must also walk through machines that detect metal; usually, what is detected is nothing more dangerous than a set of keys or metal jewelery, but it could easily be a weapon. Their luggage has to go through X-ray machines that reveal whether there are any weapons or other suspicious objects hidden.

Some airlines, like El Al, even put armed **air marshals** on board, disguised as passengers. These are very much like the guards who used to "ride shotgun" on mail and passenger coaches in the days of the Wild West in the United States. The air marshals carry special guns to deal with hijackers while the aircraft is still in flight. It is dangerous to fire guns inside an aircraft because the bullets can puncture the aircraft's outer "skin" and cause the aircraft cabin to explode or crash. Special ammunition is therefore used to avoid this dangerous hazard.

These measures all help reduce the problem of aircraft hijacking, but do not get rid of it completely. Determined hijackers manage to get on board aircraft just the same, and the taking of hostages continues today.

AIRCRAFT RESCUE: THE DIFFICULTIES

As a result, special teams of rescuers have now been trained to assault hijacked airliners, releasing the hostages and dealing with the hijackers. They have only one opportunity—after the aircraft has

A RESCUE THAT SUCCEEDED

In 1977, Arab hijackers, led by the notorious terrorist Zohair Youssef Akache, united with the German terrorist Baader-Meinhoff gang in an attempt to secure the release of gang members from prison. On October 13, four Arabs hijacked a Boeing 737 jet belonging to Lufthansa, the West German airline. It was flying 86 passengers to Germany from Palma, in the Balearic Islands (in the Mediterranean Sea).

Diverted to Rome, Akache demanded that the aircraft be refueled, or else he would blow it up. He made the same threat after the aircraft landed in Cyprus. On both occasions, the fuel was provided. Akache then forced the pilot to fly to Mogadishu, the capital of Somalia. There, a team of rescuers was waiting.

The aircraft was assaulted on the runway by 22 rescuers: 20 of them came from the Grenzchutzgruppe 9 (GSG-9), the German counterterrorist unit, and two were members of the British SAS. The SAS carried "stun" grenades, which they threw against the front of the aircraft. The four hijackers, thinking the rescue attempt was going to take place there, rushed forward to stop it, only to find that this "attack" was a trick. The rescuers entered the plane behind them and rescued the hostages, killing or capturing the hijackers.

landed at an airport. This airport is either the one chosen by the hijackers, or an airport where they have been forced to land by a shortage of fuel.

Rescuing hostages from hijacked aircraft has its own special

In 1970, Palestinian terrorists blew up three empty passenger liners in Amman, Jordan. In this picture, one of the Boeing 707s is shown exploding spectacularly.

problems. One of them is that the aircraft interiors are small, narrow, and crowded. It can be difficult to tell who is a hostage and who is a hijacker. In addition, there is always the danger that an armed rescue can result in a fire on board the aircraft. This, of course, puts the hostages at great risk, which is why flammable gases are not normally used in rescues from hijacked aircraft.

Another problem for rescuers is that the many planes flying the world's air routes are of different designs. For example, not all planes have the same type of doors. Rescue teams must know the type of door and how it opens if they are going to get into the aircraft quickly. **Jumbo jets**, such as the Boeing 747 or the Douglas DC-10, have doors with hinges on one side that swing out to let passengers get on and off the plane. The doors on the Boeing 767, however, are electronically operated and swing upward. The smaller Boeing 727 has a door at the back of the aircraft; passengers get on and off by means of a built-in stairway. These differences mean that rescue teams have to practice getting into every kind of aircraft used by the major airlines.

Sometimes, a rescue team will decide to get into an aircraft by using the **emergency doors** placed along the **fuselage** above the

Airport security staff make thorough checks to make sure that luggage is safe prior to takeoff. A dog's sensitive nose is very useful for sniffing out drugs or explosives hidden in suitcases.

WHY HIJACK AIRCRAFT?

There are several reasons why aircraft have proved to be useful targets for terrorists.

• Airlines and their aircraft are symbols of the country to which they belong. Indeed, airlines are often government-owned, and as such the aircraft are their countries' "national flag carriers." Terrorists who have a quarrel with, say, the United States, Israel, or France— all of them countries whose aircraft have been hijacked—believe they are striking a blow against the country itself.

• A hijacking, like all acts of terrorism, makes headlines across the world. It is an effective way to promote a cause.

• An aircraft in flight has a ready-made collection of hostages—the passengers and crew, none of whom can escape from a craft 30,000 feet (9,144 m) or more up in the air.

• In addition, aircraft can go anywhere in the world as long as they have enough fuel. Usually, the countries to which they want to fly are likely to be friendly toward them.

• The hijackers can threaten to kill their hostages unless their demands are met and they are given the fuel they need. This is the ultimate weapon available to the hijackers.

Left: In 1996, at Stansted Airport in England, Iraqi hijackers siezed a Sudanese aircraft in order to seek political asylum in Britain. Here, British agents enter the aircraft, wary of traps or explosives left on board, even though the hijackers had already given themselves up.

Here, passengers are forced to pass through a metal detector at O'Hare Airport in Chicago, Illinois.

wings. The best chance of success lies with using team members who are not too large and heavy; they are less likely to make the wing move or rock, and thus have a better chance of creeping along it to the emergency doors and taking the hijackers by surprise before they know what is happening.

Another way to get into an aircraft is by using ladders. Of course, doors are at different heights on different aircraft; the ladders must be the right length. They must also be strong enough to let the rescuers climb them while carrying heavy equipment and weapons. However, although rescue teams are well equipped and thoroughly practiced at getting hostages out of hijacked aircraft, they do not always manage. Sadly, it often happens that hostages are killed or injured during a rescue.

Hostage rescue is a risky business. No one can ever be sure of success because violence is usually involved and cannot be easily controlled—nervous hijackers can become violent all too easily. So a rescue team faces a difficult decision: will the hostages be in greater danger if it does not attempt a rescue, or if it does? As a rule, rescues take place only if the hijackers are so violent that the hostages are bound to be killed or injured, and rescue, however dangerous, is their only chance to survive.

An Air France A320 airbus was hijacked in France in 1994: 75 passengers were taken hostage, but were later released.

Chinese police, fire, and medical personnel combine in a mock rescue exercise in Shenzen, southern China. Note the inflatable chute that enables passengers to get to the ground quickly and safely. China has a zero-tolerance policy to air piracy.

ANTITERRORIST AND HOSTAGE-RESCUE TEAMS OF THE WORLD

Terrorism and hostage taking is a problem all over the world. Here are some of the organizations whose job it is to fight against them.

Great Britain:

Special Air Service (SAS)

Special Boat Service (SBS)

Royal Marines

France:

Groupe d'Intervention

Gendarmerie Nationale (GIGN)

Germany:

Grenzschutzgruppe 9 (GSG-9)

Kommando Spezialkraefte (KSK)

India:

National Security Guards (NSG)

Israel:

Unit 269 (Sayeret Mat'kal or General Staff Reconnaissance)

D4 (Flotilla 13, The Batmen)

Italy:

Divisione Operazioni Speciale (Special Operations Division— NOCS)

Gruppo Intervento Speciale (Special Intervention Group— GIS)

Russia:

Omon (The Black Berets)

Alpha Group A (AL'FA)

Spetzgruppa Vympel (Special Operations Unit—VYMPEL)

United States:

FBI Hostage Rescue Team (HRT)

Delta Force (U.S. Army)

Hostage Rescue Unit (HRU)

SEAL Team 6 or DevGroup (Naval Special Warfare Development Group, U.S. Navy)

GLOSSARY

Abseil (v.): to travel down a rope

Acrophobia: a fear of heights

Air marshal: armed guard traveling on an aircraft to protect the passengers and crew; the air marshal is often disguised as a passenger

Aquaphobia: a fear of water

Bulkhead: partitions that divide the sections of a ship

Conquistadors: these were 16th-century Spanish adventurers who conquered much of South and Central America and claimed the land there for the Spanish crown

Crusade: a series of wars fought by Christians against Muslims between 1196 and 1304, in or around the Holy Land (now Israel)

Culvert: a large drainage channel that runs alongside a road or building

Diversion: action that takes attention away from what is happening elsewhere

Endoscope: an instrument for viewing the internal parts of the body

Emergency doors: doors in a building or aircraft designed to be used for a quick escape in the event of an emergency

Fuselage: the body of an aircraft

Gulley: a deep artificial channel

Hijack: to take unlawful control of a ship, train, aircraft, or other form of transport

Insertion: getting into a place where hostages are being held

Jumbo jet: a large jet aircraft that can hold up to 400 passengers at one time

Obstacle course: a series of tests with blocks or difficulties that have to be overcome

Powers of observation: the ability to notice what is happening in a situation

Ransom: money that is given to kidnappers in exchange for a person or persons

Sniper: a gunman or -woman who can hit targets accurately

Stake out (v.): to surround a site where criminals are holed up, with or without hostages

Stern: the rear end of a ship

Stethoscope: a instrument used to listen to what is happening inside a building

Terrorist: a person using violence and terror to achieve their aims

Trainee: a person who is learning how to do a job

CHRONOLOGY

1193–1194: King Richard I (Richard the Lionheart) is held hostage for ransom by Duke Leopold of Austria.

1931: February 21, first known aircraft hijacking in Peru; one hostage taken.

1932: Kidnap and murder of the baby son of Charles Lindbergh, the first man to fly alone across the Atlantic in 1927.

1968: Hijack of an El Al aircraft by the Popular Front for the Liberation of Palestine; the 32 passengers on board are held for five weeks before being freed; the hijackers escape.

1970: Canadian government minister Pierre Laporte is kidnapped and murdered.

1976: Israeli special forces rescue 101 Israeli and Jewish hostages held at Entebbe Airport, Uganda, by terrorists in the name of the Palestine Liberation Organization (PLO).

1977: South Moluccan terrorists hijack a train in the Netherlands and hold 94 passengers hostage for three weeks.

1978: Kidnap and murder of Aldo Moro, Italian presidential candidate.

1980: SAS rescues hostages from the Iranian Embassy, London; the rescue is covered live on international television.

1983: FBI's Hostage Rescue Team is formed.

1985: Italian cruise liner *Achille Lauro*, with 454 passengers and crew on board, is seized by four terrorists; one hostage is murdered; two of the terrorists are later put on trial and imprisoned; the other two are freed.

1987: Terry Waite, special representative of the Archbishop of Canterbury, England, negotiates the release of many hostages taken by terrorists in Lebanon; but in January of the same year, Waite was himself taken hostage and not released until November 1991.

1987: The FBI's Hostage Rescue Team helps to free 124 hostages taken by inmates at Atlanta Prison, USA.

1993: The FBI's Hostage Rescue Team is involved in the siege of the Branch Davidian religious group at Waco, Texas, who held children as hostages; the siege ended in a fire in which 87 people, including 17 children, died.

1996: December 17, the Japanese ambassador's home in Lima, Peru, was surrounded by Marxist rebels, who take the 600 party guests hostage; the last 74 hostages were not rescued until April 1997.

FURTHER INFORMATION

USEFUL WEB SITES

For a history of the SAS: www.guardian.co.uk/waronteror/story

For information about Delta Force (U.S. Army): www.special-forces.net/Delta_Force

For the Israeli raid on Entebbe (Uganda) in 1976: www.claremont.org/precepts

Rescue One SWAT (police): rescue1.com/swat6.htm

FBI Hostage Rescue Team (HRT): www.specialoperations.com

Federal Bureau of Investigation (FBI) Special Operations and Response Units; Hostage Rescue Team (HRT); Critical Incident Response Group (CIRG); The FBI's Critical Incident Response Group (CIRG): www.specialoperations.com/Domestic/FBI

The Navy SEALs, Army Rangers, and the Army's SFOD-Delta (Delta Force): www.geocities.com

Counterterrorism guide page: www.angelfire.com/nt/tic6/strategys/strategyscscom

Counterterrorists groups of the world: www.specwarnet.com

FURTHER READING

Coulson, Danny O. and Elaine Shannon. *No Heroes: Inside the FBI's Secret Counter-terror Force*. New York: Pocket Books, 1999.

McNab, Chris. *Hostage Rescue with the SAS. Elite Forces, Survival Guides*. Philadelphia: Mason Crest, 2002.

Thompson, Leroy. *Hostage Rescue Manual*. Pennsylvania: Greenhill Books, 2001.

Whitcombe, Christopher. *Cold Zero: Inside the FBI Hostage Rescue Team*. Boston: Little Brown, 2001.

ABOUT THE AUTHOR

Brenda Ralph Lewis is a prolific writer of books, articles, television documentary scripts, and other materials on history, royalty, military subjects, aviation, and philately. Her writing includes many books on ancient history, culture, and life; and books on World War II, including *The Hitler Youth: The Hitlerjugend in Peace and War 1933-1945* (2000), *Women At War* (2001), and *The Story of Anne Frank* (2001). She has also written or contributed to numerous books for children, including *The Aztecs* (1999), *Stamps! A Young Philatelist's Guide* (1998), and *Ritual Sacrifice: A History* (2002). She lives in Buckinghamshire, England.

INDEX